MW00896661

NO LONGER PROPERTY OF
SEATTLE PUBLIC LIBRARY

CAT ON THE BUS

CAT ON THE BUS

ARAM KIM

HOLIDAY HOUSE / NEW YORK

FOR MY
FAMILY
AND
HORANG

Copyright © 2016 by Aram Kim. • All Rights Reserved • HOLIDAY HOUSE is registered in the U.S. Patent and Trademark Office.

Printed and bound in April 2016 at Tien Wah Press, Johor Bahru, Johor, Malaysia. • The artwork was made with pastels and color pencils on paper and then
digitally composited and colored. • www.holidayhouse.com • First Edition • 1 3 5 7 9 10 8 6 4 2
Library of Congress Cataloging-in-Publication Data
Names: Kim, Aram, author. • Title: Cat on the bus / Aram Kim. • Description: First edition. | New York : Holiday House, [2016] | Summary:
"Using onomatopoeia, this almost wordless story tells of a homeless cat • who finds shelter on a bus where she meets a cat-loving Asian grandfather"— Provided by publisher.
Identifiers: LCCN 2015041859 | ISBN 9780823436477 (hardcover) • Subjects: | CYAC: Cats—Fiction. | Human-animal relationships—Fiction.
Classification: LCC PZ7.1.K548 Cat 2016 | DDC [E]—dc23 LC record available at http://lccn.loc.gov/2015041859

CLACK
Clang
Rattle
Clatter!

Scat, cat!

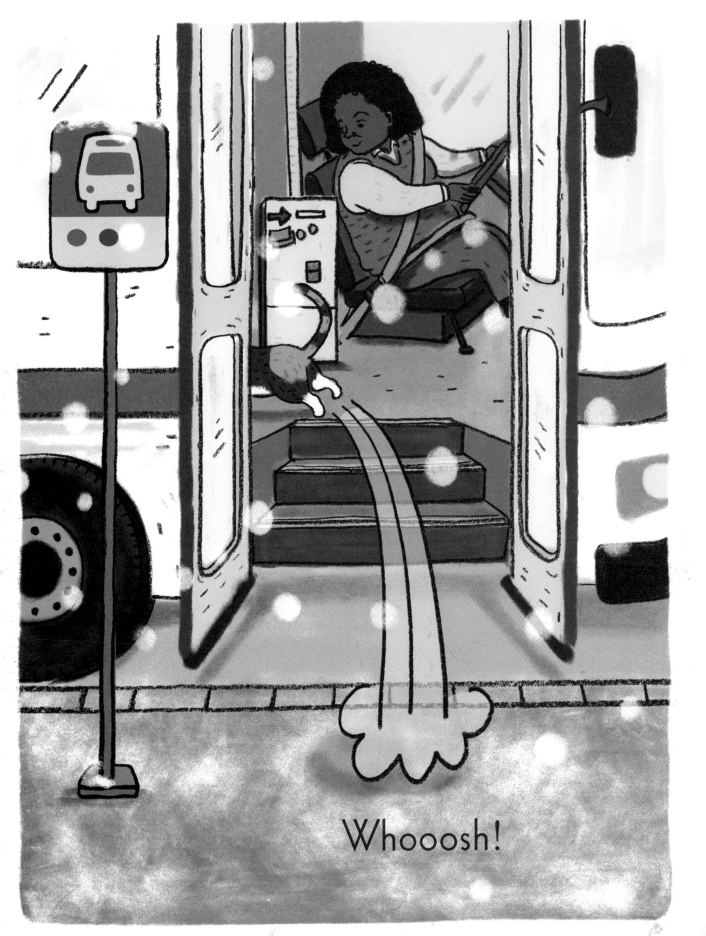

Whooosh!

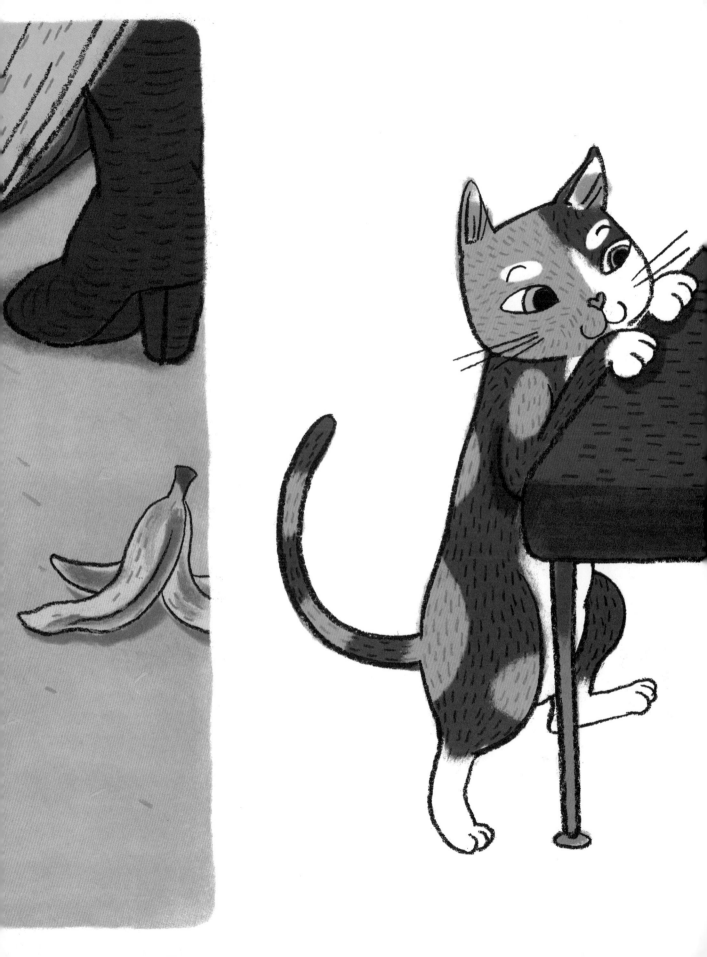

Purrrrrrrrr

Purrrrrrr-fect